I0458180

Deathly Visitors

Visitors

APPARITIONS AT OR
AFTER DEATH

By

St. John D. Seymour

Copyright © 2011 Read Books Ltd.
This book is copyright and may not be
reproduced or copied in any way without
the express permission of the publisher in writing

British Library Cataloguing-in-Publication Data
A catalogue record for this book is available from
the British Library

Contents

Page
No.

St. John D. Seymour

St. John Drelincourt Seymour was born in the second half of the 19th century in Ireland. Around 1913, he came to realize that although Ireland was replete with collections of folklore and fairy-tales, the country's rich tradition of ghost stories remained largely untapped. Working with friend Harry L. Neligan, Seymour set out to correct this. The two of them put out a request for anecdotes in the newspapers of the day, and compiled the stories they received in what is now Seymour's most well-known 'non-fiction' work, *True Irish Ghost Stories* (1914). Around the same time, Seymour published his other more popular titles, *Irish Witchcraft and Demonology* and *Haunted Houses in or Near Dublin*.

IT has been said by a very eminent literary man that the accounts of the appearance of people at or shortly after the moment of death make very dull reading as a general rule. This may be; they are certainly not so lengthy, or full of detail, as the accounts of haunted houses—nor could such be expected. In our humble opinion, however, they are full of interest, and open up problems of telepathy and thought-transference to which the solutions may not be found for years to come. That people have seen the image of a friend or relative at the moment of dissolution, sometimes in the ordinary garb of life, sometimes with symbolical accompaniments, or that they have been made acquainted in some abnormal manner with the fact that such a one has passed away, seems to be demonstrated beyond all reasonable doubt. But we would hasten to add that such appearances are not a proof of existence after death, nor can they be regarded in the light of special interventions of a merciful Providence. Were they either they would surely occur far oftener. The question is, Why do they occur at all? As it is, the majority of them seem to happen for no particular reason, and are often seen by persons who have little or no connection with the deceased, not by their nearest and dearest, as one might expect. It is supposed they are *veridical* hallucinations, *i.e.* ones which correspond with objective events at a distance, and are caused by a telepathic impact conveyed from the mind of an absent agent to the mind of the percipient.

From their nature they fall under different heads. The majority of them occur at what may most conveniently be described as the time of death, though how closely they approximate in reality to the instant of the Great Change it is impossible to say. So we have divided this chapter into three groups:

(1) Appearances at the time of death (as explained above).

(2) Appearances clearly *after* the time of death.

(3) In this third group we hope to give some curious tales of appearances some time *before* death.

Group I

We commence this group with stories in which the phenomena connected with the respective deaths were not perceived as representations of the human form. In the first of these only sounds were heard. It was sent as a personal experience by the Archdeacon of Limerick, (the late) Very Rev. J. A. Haydn, LL.D. " In the year 1879 there lived in the picturesque village of Adare, at a distance of about eight or nine miles from my residence, a District Inspector named ——, with whom I enjoyed a friendship of the most intimate and fraternal kind. At the time I write of, Mrs. —— was expecting the arrival of their third child. She was a particularly tiny and fragile woman, and much anxiety was felt as to the result of the impending event. He and she had very frequently spent pleasant days at my house, with all the apartments of which they were thoroughly acquainted—a fact of importance in this narrative.

" On Wednesday, October 17, 1879, I had a very jubilant letter from my friend, announcing that the expected event had successfully happened on the previous day, and that all was progressing satisfactorily. On the night of the following Wednesday, October 22, I retired to bed at about ten o'clock. My wife, the children, and two maidservants were all sleeping upstairs, and I had a small bed in my study, which was on the ground floor. The house was shrouded in darkness, and the only sound that broke the silence was the ticking of the hall clock.

" I was quietly preparing to go to sleep, when I was much surprised at hearing, with the most unquestionable distinctness, the sound of light, hurried footsteps, exactly suggestive of those of an active, restless young female, coming in from the hall door and traversing the hall. They then, apparently with some hesitation, followed the passage leading to the study door, on arriving at which they stopped. I then heard the sound of a light, agitated hand apparently searching for the handle of the door. By this time, being quite sure that my wife had come down and wanted to speak to me, I sat up in bed, and called to her by name, asking what was the matter. As there was no reply, and the sounds had ceased, I struck a match, lighted a candle, and opened the door. No one was visible or audible. I went upstairs, found all the doors shut and every one asleep. Greatly puzzled, I returned to the study and went to bed, leaving the candle alight. Immediately the whole performance was circumstantially repeated, but *this* time the handle of the door was grasped by the invisible hand, and *partly* turned, then relinquished. I started out of bed and renewed my previous search, with equally futile results. The clock struck eleven, and from that time all disturbances ceased.

" On Friday morning I received a letter stating that Mrs. —— had died at about midnight on the previous Wednesday. I hastened off to Adare and had an interview with my bereaved friend. With one item of our conversation I will close. He told me that his wife sank rapidly on Wednesday, until when night came on she became delirious. She spoke incoherently, as if revisiting scenes and places once familiar. ' She thought she was in *your* house,' he said, ' and was apparently holding a conversation with *you*, as she used to keep silence at intervals as if listening to your replies.' I asked him if he could possibly remember the hour at which the imaginary conversation took place. He replied that, curiously enough, he could tell it accurately, as he had looked at his watch, and found the time between half-past ten and eleven o'clock—the exact time of the mysterious manifestations heard by me."

The daughter of a well-known clergyman in the Diocese of Cork has sent us the following account of sounds at the time of death being heard by two people. She furnished us with some names, but on consideration we have thought it best not to publish them.

" On the morning of Saturday, July 26, 1876, my father went into the study of his Rectory in Co. Cork, and commenced to read. His attention was soon diverted by a constant recurring noise that seemed to be over his head: it sounded like a tapping, or perhaps it would be more accurate to say it resembled the sound made by a ball being dropped from a height—pop, pop, pop!— gradually growing fainter until it died away, and then, after a pause, beginning again.

" As the nursery was overhead his study he naturally assumed that it was a noise made by the children, and tried not to notice it, though at the same time he felt curiously upset and restless. About twelve o'clock he could stand it no longer, and went upstairs to where his wife was. On his telling her the reason for his coming she informed him that the children had been out for the entire morning. They went together into the deserted nursery, and listened; she could hear nothing, but he did, and continued to hear it at intervals during the entire day, until it ceased towards night.

"The cook, who was down in the basement, assured her mistress that she had got a terrible fright that morning, for she had heard a man's voice, which she did not recognise, calling ' Mary! Mary! '

"Shortly after my father heard very sad news, which threw some light on the mysterious occurrence. The former occupant of the house had been made a Bishop some ten years previously. He had fallen ill with fever, and in a moment of delirium had inflicted such injuries upon himself that he died in Dublin the morning the sounds were heard. His wife's name was Mary; his bedroom had been the room over the study, which we used as a nursery, while in the basement he had fitted up a workshop."

We shall now give two stories in which the appearance of light is an indication of the moment of death. The first of these is not a first-hand experience; it was sent to the writer by the Rev. H. R. B. Gillespie, to whom it was told by the percipient.

The eldest brother of a family lived at home

most of his life. The youngest brother married, and went out in the world, but subsequently fell into ill-health, and returned with his wife and son to stay with his father. While there he became so ill that for months he was confined to bed, and there was no hope of recovery. Finally he died in the month of July.

On the evening of his death his eldest brother was out walking in the fields accompanied by an old nurse who had been with the members of the family since the time they were children. As the brother drew near the house he noticed what he described as " rays like the rays of the setting sun coming round the corner of the house ". From where he was standing he could not see the window of his brother's bedroom; it was in the front of the house, and he was at the side. But his impression was, that the rays came from the window round the corner, and that in the centre of them was a " misty light ", which came towards him till it almost reached the earth. He felt very uneasy as the light came nearer and nearer, but when it had almost reached to where he was standing " it shot up like a shooting-star, only going the wrong way ".

He said to the nurse, " J. is dead! " and walked on quickly towards the front door, which one of his sisters was just opening in order to go out and look for him. He said to her, " You need not tell me the sad news—I know he has just died! " It was then nearly 9.30 P.M. The nurse did not see the rays of light at all, and only heard the elder brother say that the sick man had passed away.

A lady sends the following personal experience: "I had a cousin in the country who was not very strong, and on one occasion she desired me to go to her, and accompany her to K——. I consented to do so, and arranged a day to go and meet her: this was in the month of February. The evening before I was to go, I was sitting by the fire in my small parlour about 5 P.M. There was no light in the room except what proceeded from the fire. Beside the fireplace was an arm-chair, where my cousin usually sat when she was with me. Suddenly that chair was illuminated by a light so intensely bright that it actually seemed to *heave* under it, though the remainder of the room remained in semi-darkness. I called out in amazement, 'What has happened to the chair?' In a moment the light vanished, and the chair was as before. In the morning I heard that my cousin had died about the same time that I saw the light."

Canon W. F. Johnstone, of Bansha Rectory, Tipperary, sends an account of an appearance at death which was told to him by his father, the late St. George Johnstone. It marks a transition stage between the stories that precede and follow it in this chapter.

"Many years ago, when I was quite a small boy, my father, who was a keen astronomer, was out one fine moonlight night in the late autumn indulging in his favourite hobby, when he observed a curious isolated cloud or mist, globular in shape, resting at a distance of about one hundred yards on the broad flatly trimmed hedge which bordered the walk on which he was standing. He was wondering what it might be, when, to his surprise, it began to move slowly along the flat top of the broad hedge as if on a path, until it came to rest within a few yards of him. Then, to his utter amazement, the outlines of a face began to appear in the centre of this circular ball of mist, and gradually developed into the likeness of his mother's countenance, set, as it were, in a framework of mist. He saw this face distinctly and for the space of some seconds, when it broke into a smile, and in a moment the vision dissolved. His mother died on the day, and at the very hour, on which the globular mist appeared.

" This is, as far as my memory serves me—and the story made a deep impression upon me at the time — the exact account given me by my father years after it took place. I believe it to be true in every particular. My father was a cultured, highly educated man, intensely practical, and not at all a dreamer of dreams."

The following story is sent by Mr. F. C. Pilkington:

In the year of the dreadful cholera a certain County family, who are still well known there, resided in Clare. When the plague was at its worst the female members of this family were sent for greater safety to a remote part of the County, where they had a summer residence, at which they were wont to spend some months every year.

There were either four or five sisters, one of whom was the writer's grandmother. A brother was a doctor practising in Dublin, and he came to Ennis in the hope of being able to give some medical assistance to the sufferers. The people were dying in hundreds, and the local doctors were terribly overworked and unable to cope with the ravages of the dread disease.

The sisters learned that their brother (Charles was his name) had arrived in Ennis, and they looked forward to a visit from him before he returned to Dublin.

One night they all felt strangely uneasy, and were possessed with that peculiar sense of impending evil which most people must have experienced at one time or another. One of the sisters decided she would go upstairs and lie down, but the others preferred to remain up, so pulled their chairs round the fire and prepared for an all-night sitting.

Presently they heard the front gate open and the sound of a horse's hoofs galloping on the short drive from the public road to the house. They all stood up to go to the door, and in the hall met the sister who had gone to lie down and who had also heard the horse. The same idea occurred to each at once, that it was Charles, who had ridden from Ennis to pay them a surprise visit.

TRUE IRISH GHOST STORIES

The horse could now be heard almost at the door, which the sisters flung open with a cry of welcome on their lips. When the door was opened there was nothing to be seen or heard. Dead silence reigned. Terror - stricken now they closed the door and returned to the sitting-room. The clock on the mantelpiece showed the time to be 12.30, and, as sleep for any of them was now more impossible than ever, they huddled together over the fire during the dreary hours before the dawn of day.

At long last dawn came, and with it a messenger who had ridden on horseback from Ennis.

This was the message which the sisters read in the light of the early dawn: " Charles died at 12.30 this morning." He had fallen a victim to the plague.

We now come to the ordinary type, *i.e.* where a figure appears. The following tale illustrates a point we have already alluded to, namely, that the apparition is sometimes seen by a disinterested person, and *not* by those whom one would naturally expect should see it. A lady writes as follows: " At Island Magee is the Knowehead Lonan, a long, hilly, narrow road, bordered on either side by high thorn-hedges and fields. Twenty years ago, when I was a young girl, I used to go to the post office at the Knowehead on Sunday mornings down the Lonan, taking the dogs for the run. One Sunday, as I had got to the top of the hill on my return journey, I looked back, and saw a man walking rapidly after me, but still a good way off. I hastened my steps, for the day was muddy, and I did not want him to see me in a bedraggled state. But he seemed to come on so fast as to be soon close behind me, and I wondered he did not pass me, so on we went, I never turning to look back. About a quarter of a mile farther on I met A. B. on ' Dick's Brae ', on her way to church or Sunday school, and stopped to speak to her. I wanted to ask who the man was, but he seemed to be so close that I did not like to do so, and expected he had passed. When I moved on, I was surprised to find he was still following me, while my dogs were lagging behind with downcast heads and drooping tails.

" I then passed a cottage where C. D. was out feeding her fowls. I spoke to her, and then feeling that there was no longer any one behind, looked back, and saw the man standing with her. I would not have paid any attention to the matter had not A. B. been down at our house that afternoon, and I casually asked her:

" ' Who was the man who was just behind me when I met you on Dick's Brae? '

" ' What man? ' said she; and noting my look of utter astonishment, added, ' I give you my word I never met a soul but yourself from the time I left home till I went down to Knowehead Lonan.'

" Next day C. D. came to work for us, and I asked her who was the man who was standing beside her after I passed her on Sunday.

"'Naebody!' she replied, 'I saw naebody but yoursel'.'

"It all seemed very strange, and so they thought too. About three weeks later news came that C. D.'s only brother, a sailor, was washed overboard that Sunday morning."

The following story is not a first-hand experience, but is sent by the gentleman to whom it was related by the percipient. The latter said to him:

"I was sitting in this same chair I am in at present one evening, when I heard a knock at the front door. I went myself to see who was there, and on opening the door saw my old friend P. Q. standing outside with his gun in his hand. I was surprised at seeing him, but asked him to come in and have something. He came inside the porch into the lamplight, and stood there for a few moments; then he muttered something about being sorry he had disturbed me, and that he was on his way to see his brother, Colonel Q., who lived about a mile farther on. Without any further explanation he walked away towards the gate into the dusk.'

"I was greatly surprised and perplexed, but as he had gone I sat down again by the fire. About an hour later another knock came to the door, and I again went out to see who was there. On opening it I found P. Q.'s groom holding a horse, and he asked me where he was, as he had missed his way in the dark, and did not know the locality.

I told him, and then asked him where he was going, and why, and he replied that his master was dead (at his own house about nine miles away), and that he had been sent to announce the news to Colonel Q."

Canon J. C. Trotter, formerly Incumbent of Ardrahan, sends the following:

" My maternal grandmother lived with my father and mother in Belfast. She was dying, and my mother was sitting up with her. The old woman's hair had become dishevelled through tossing about on her pillow, and in order to get something to keep it tidy my mother went up to a bedroom on a higher floor in which my father (an invalid) was sleeping. She glanced towards his bed, saw that he was asleep, opened a drawer gently, and took out a piece of ribbon with which she tied up her mother's hair.

" Very shortly after this the sick woman passed away. My mother went up immediately to my father's room to acquaint him of the fact. She found him awake, and he at once remarked on her entry:

" ' I know what you have come to tell me—mother is gone! '

" ' Yes! ' replied my mother. ' But how did you know? '

" ' I saw her! ' was the answer. ' She said, " John, I am crossing the Jordan! " I asked, " What is the prospect, mother? " She replied, " Bright! Bright! Bright! " And each time she repeated that word her face grew less distinct. But what struck me as remarkable was, that her hair was confined by a ribbon!'" Canon Trotter adds that his father named the colour of the ribbon, and that it exactly corresponded to the colour of that one with which his mother had tied up the dying woman's hair.

Miss Grene, of Grene Park, Co. Tipperary, relates a story which was told her by the late Miss ——, sister of a former Dean of Cashel. The latter, an old lady, stated that one time she was staying with a friend in a house in the suburbs of Dublin. In front of the house was the usual grass plot, divided into two by a short gravel path which led down to a gate which opened on to the street. She and her friend were one day engaged in needlework in one of the front rooms, when they heard the gate opening, and on looking out the window they saw an elderly gentleman of their acquaintance coming up the path. As he approached the door both exclaimed: "Oh, how good of him to come and see us!" As he was not shown into the sitting-room, one of them rang the bell, and said to the maid when she appeared, "You have not let Mr. So-and-so in; he is at the door for some little time." The maid went to the hall door, and returned to say that there was no one there. Next day they learnt that he had died just at the hour that they had seen him coming up the path.

The following tale contains a curious point. A

good many years ago the Rev. Henry Morton, now dead, held a curacy in Ireland. He had to pass through the graveyard when leaving his house to visit the parishioners. One beautiful moonlight night he was sent for to visit a sick person, and was accompanied by his brother, a medical man, who was staying with him. After performing the religious duty they returned through the churchyard, and were chatting about various matters when to their astonishment a figure passed them, both seeing it. This figure left the path, and went in among the gravestones, and then disappeared. They could not understand this at all, so they went to the spot where the disappearance took place, but, needless to say, could find nobody after the most careful search. Next morning they heard that the person visited had died just after their departure, while the most marvellous thing of all was that the burial took place at the very spot where they had seen the phantom disappear.

The Rev. D. B. Knox communicates the following : In a girls' boarding-school several years ago two of the boarders were sleeping in a large double-bedded room with two doors. About two o'clock in the morning the girls were awakened by the entrance of a tall figure in clerical attire, the face of which they did not see. They screamed in fright, but the figure moved in a slow and stately manner past their beds and out the other door. It also appeared to one or two of the other boarders, and seemed to be looking for some one. At length it reached the bed of one who was evidently known to it. The girl woke up and recognised her father. He did not speak, but gazed for a few moments at his daughter, and then vanished. Next morning a telegram was handed to her which communicated the sad news that her father had died on the previous evening at the hour when he appeared to her.

Here is a story of a very old type. It occurred a good many years ago. A gentleman named Miller resided in Co. Wexford, while his friend and former schoolfellow, Mr. Scott, lived in the North of Ireland. This long friendship led them to visit at each other's houses from time to time, but for Mr. Miller there was a deep shadow of sorrow over these otherwise happy moments, for, while he enjoyed the most enlightened religious opinions, his friend was an unbeliever. The last time they were together Mr. Scott said, " My dear friend, let us solemnly promise that whichever of us shall die first shall appear to the other after death, if it be possible." " Let it be so, if God will," replied Mr. Miller. One morning some time after, about three o'clock, the latter was awakened by a brilliant light in his bedroom; he imagined that the house must be on fire, when he felt what seemed to be a hand laid on him, and heard his friend's voice say distinctly, " There is a God, just but terrible in His judgements ", and all again was dark. Mr. Miller at once wrote down this remarkable experience. Two days later he received a letter announcing Mr. Scott's death on the night, and at the hour, that he had seen the light in his room.

The above leads us on to the famous " Beresford Ghost ", which is generally regarded as holding the same position relative to Irish ghosts that Dame Alice Kyteler used to hold with respect to Irish witches and wizards. The story is so well known, and has been published so often, that only a brief allusion is necessary, with the added information that the best version is to be found in Andrew Lang's *Dreams and Ghosts*, chapter viii. (Silver Library Edition). Lord Tyrone appeared after death one night to Lady Beresford at Gill Hall, in accordance with a promise (as in the last story) made in early life. He assured her that the religion as revealed by Jesus Christ was the only true one (both he and Lady Beresford had been brought up Deists), told her that she was *enceinte* and would bear a son, and also foretold her second marriage, and the time of her death. In proof whereof he drew the bed-hangings through an iron hook, wrote his name in her pocket-book, and finally placed a hand cold as marble on her wrist, at which the sinews shrunk up. To the day of her death Lady Beresford wore a black ribbon round her wrist; this was taken off before her burial, and it was found the nerves were withered, and the sinews shrunken, as she had previously described to her children.

GROUP II

We now come to some stories of apparitions seen some time after the hour of death. The late Canon Ross-Lewin, of Limerick, furnished the following incident in his own family. " My uncle, John Dillon Ross-Lewin, lieutenant in the 30th Regiment, was mortally wounded at Inkerman on November 5, 1854, and died on the morning of the 6th. He appeared that night to his mother, who was then on a visit in Co. Limerick, intimating his death, and indicating where the wound was. The strangest part of the occurrence is, that when news came later on of the casualties at Inkerman, the first account as to the wound did *not* correspond with what the apparition indicated to his mother, but the final account did. Mrs. Ross-Lewin was devoted to her son, and he was equally attached to her; she, as the widow of a field officer who fought at Waterloo, would be able to comprehend the battle scene, and her mind at the time was centred on the events of the Crimean War."

A clergyman, who desires that all names be suppressed, sends the following: " In my wife's father's house a number of female servants were kept, of whom my wife, before she was married, was in charge. On one occasion the cook took ill with appendicitis, and was operated on in the Infirmary, where I attended her as hospital chaplain. She died, however, and was buried by her friends. Some days after the funeral my wife was standing at a table in the kitchen which was so placed that any person standing at it could see into the passage outside the kitchen, if the door happened to be open. [The narrator enclosed a rough plan which made the whole story perfectly clear.] She was standing one day by herself at the table, and the door was open. This was in broad daylight, about eleven o'clock in the morning in the end of February or beginning of March. She was icing a cake, and therefore was hardly thinking of ghosts. Suddenly she looked up from her work, and glanced through the open kitchen door into the passage leading past the servants' parlour into the dairy. She saw quite distinctly the figure of the deceased cook pass towards the dairy; she was dressed in the ordinary costume she used to wear in the mornings, and seemed in every respect quite normal. My wife was not, at the moment, in the least shocked or surprised, but, on the contrary, she followed, and searched in the dairy, into which she was just in time to see her skirts disappearing. Needless to say, nothing was visible."

The late Canon Courtenay Moore, M.A., Rector of Mitchelstown, contributed a personal experience. " It was about eighteen years ago— I cannot fix the exact date—that Samuel Penrose returned to this parish from the Argentine. He was getting on so well abroad that he would have remained there, but his wife fell ill, and for her sake he returned to Ireland. He was a carpenter by trade, and his former employer was glad to take him into his service again. Sam was a very respectable man of sincere religious feelings. Soon after his return he met with one or two rather severe accidents, and had a strong impression that a fatal one would happen him before long; and so it came to pass. A scaffolding gave way one day, and precipitated him on to a flagged stone floor. He did not die immediately, but his injuries proved fatal. He died in a Cork hospital soon after his admission: I went to Cork to officiate at his funeral. About noon the next day I was standing at my hall door, and the form of poor Sam, the upper half of it, seemed to pass before me. He looked peaceful and happy—it was a momentary vision, but perfectly distinct. The truncated appearance puzzled me very much, until some time after I read a large book by F. W. H. Myers, in which he made a scientific analysis and induction of such phenomena, and said that they were almost universally seen in this half-length form. I do not profess to explain what I saw: its message, if it had a message, seemed to be that poor Sam was at last at rest and in peace."

A story somewhat similar to the above was related to us, in which the apparition seems certainly to have been sent with a definite purpose. Two maiden ladies, whom we shall call Miss A. X. and Miss B. Y., lived together for a good many years. As one would naturally expect, they were close friends, and had the most intimate relations with each other, both being extremely religious women.

APPARITIONS AFTER DEATH

In process of time Miss B. Y. died, and after death Miss A. X. formed the impression, for some unknown reason, that all was not well with her friend —that, in fact, her soul was not at rest. This thought caused her great uneasiness and trouble of mind. One day she was sitting in her arm-chair thinking over this and crying bitterly. Suddenly she saw in front of her a brilliant light, in the midst of which was her friend's face, easily recognisable, but transfigured, and wearing a most beatific expression. She rushed towards it with her arms outstretched, crying, " Oh! B., why have you come? " At this the apparition faded away, but ever after Miss A. X. was perfectly tranquil in mind with respect to her friend's salvation.

A lady has sent the following experience of her son, in which the latter beheld the apparition of a person who had no connection with him. It may be that the dying man had some vivid thoughts of his old home which were telepathically conveyed across half the globe, and so caused the vision or the dream—whichever we choose to call it.

" One night my son woke up and saw leaning over his bed an old man with a long grey beard. He never mentioned this appearance until the following night when we and some friends were sitting round the fire. Amongst the company was the gentleman who had lived in the house before us. As soon as my son had related his experience that gentleman exclaimed, ' Why, that seems very like old H.! He lived in this house before I came to it, and subsequently went to America.' We thought no more of the matter, but a week later a cable came from America to say that old man had died. It seems very strange, for neither my son nor any of my family had ever seen that old man, and yet my son described him so plainly that people who had known him said it could be none other than he."

This group may be brought to a conclusion by a story sent by Mr. T. MacFadden. It is not a personal experience, but happened to his father, and in an accompanying letter he states that he often heard the latter describe the incidents related therein, and that he certainly saw the ghost.

" The island of Inishinny, which is the scene of this story, is one of the most picturesque islands on the Donegal coast. With the islands of Gola and Inismaan it forms a perfectly natural harbour and safe anchorage for ships during storms. About Christmas some forty or fifty years ago a small sailing-ship put into Gola Roads (as this anchorage is called) during a prolonged storm, and the captain and two men had to obtain provisions from Bunbeg, as, owing to their being detained so long, their supply was almost exhausted. They had previously visited the island on several occasions, and made themselves at home with the people from the mainland, who were temporarily resident upon it.

" The old bar at its best was never very safe for navigation, and this evening it was in its element, as with every storm it presented one boiling, seething mass of foam. The inhabitants of the island saw the frail small boat from the ship securely inside the bar, and prophesied some dire calamity should the captain and the two sailors venture to return to the ship that night. But the captain and his companions, having secured sufficient provisions, decided (as far as I can remember the story), even in spite of the entreaties of those on shore, to return to the ship. The storm was increasing, and what with their scanty knowledge of the intricacies of the channel, and the darkness of the night, certain it was the next morning their craft was found washed ashore on the island, and the body of the captain was discovered by the first man who made the round of the shore looking for logs of timber, or other useful articles washed ashore from wrecks. The bodies of the two sailors were never recovered, and word was sent immediately to the captain's wife in Derry, who came in a few days and gave directions for the disposal of her husband's corpse.

" The island was only temporarily inhabited by a few people who had cattle and horses grazing there for some weeks in the year, and after this catastrophe they felt peculiarly lonely, and sought refuge from their thoughts by all spending the evening together in one house. This particular evening they were all seated round the fire having a chat, when they heard steps approaching the door. Though the approach was fine, soft sand, yet the steps were audible as if coming on hard ground. They knew there was no one on the island save the few who were sitting quietly round the fire, and so in eager expectation they faced round to the door. What was their amazement when the door opened and a tall, broad-shouldered man appeared and filled the whole doorway—and that man the captain who had been buried several days previously. He wore the identical suit in which he had often visited the island, and even the " cheese-cutter " cap, so common a feature of sea-faring men's apparel, was not wanting. All were struck dumb with terror, and a woman who sat in a corner opposite the door, exclaimed in Irish in a low voice to my father:

" ' O God! Patrick, there's the captain.'

" My father, recovering from the first shock, when he saw feminine courage finding expression in words, said in Irish to the apparition:

" ' Come in! '

" They were so certain of the appearance that they addressed him in his own language, as they invariably talked Irish in the district in those days. But no sooner had he uttered the invitation than the figure, without the least word or sign, moved back, and disappeared from their view. They rushed out, but could discover no sign of any living person within the confines of the island. Such is the true account of an accident by which three men lost their lives, and the ghostly sequel, in which one of them appeared to the eyes of four people, two of whom are yet alive and can vouch for the accuracy of this narrative."

GROUP III

We now come to the third group of this chapter, in which we shall relate two first-hand experiences of tragedies being actually witnessed some time before they happened, as well as a reliable second-hand story of an apparition being seen two days before the death occurred. The first of these is sent by a lady, the percipient, who desires that her name be suppressed; with it was enclosed a letter from a gentleman who stated that he could testify to the truth of the following facts:

" The morning of May 18, 1902, was one of the worst that ever dawned in Killarney. All through the day a fierce nor'-wester raged, and huge white-crested waves, known locally as ' The O'Donoghue's white horses', beat on the shores of Lough Leane. Then followed hail-showers such as I have never seen before or since. Hailstones quite as large as small marbles fell with such rapidity and seemed so hard that the glass in the windows of the room in which I stood appeared to be about to break into fragments every moment. I remained at the window, gazing out on the turbulent waters of the lake. Sometimes a regular fog appeared, caused by the terrible downpour of rain and the fury of the gale.

" During an occasional lull I could see the

islands plainly looming in the distance. In one of these clear intervals, the time being about 12.30 P.M., five friends of mine were reading in the room in which I stood. 'Quick! quick!' I cried. 'Is that a boat turned over?' My friends all ran to the windows, but could see nothing. I persisted, however, and said, 'It is on its side, with the keel turned towards us, and it is empty.' Still none of my friends could see anything. I then ran out, and got one of the men-servants to go down to a gate, about one hundred yards nearer the lake than where I stood. He had a powerful telescope, and remained with great difficulty in the teeth of the storm with his glass for several minutes, but could see nothing. When he returned another man took his place, but he also failed to see anything.

"I seemed so distressed that those around me kept going backwards and forwards to the windows, and then asked me what was the size of the boat I had seen. I gave them the exact size, measuring by landmarks. They then assured me that I must be absolutely wrong, as it was on rare occasions that a 'party' boat, such as the one I described, could venture on the lakes on such a day. Therefore there were seven persons who thought I was wrong in what I had seen. I still contended that I saw the boat, the length of which I described, as plainly as possible.

"The day wore on, and evening came. The incident was apparently more or less forgotten by all but me, until, at 8 A.M. on the following morning, when the maid brought up tea, her first words were, ' Ah, miss, is it not terrible about the accident! ' Naturally I said, ' What accident, Mary? ' She replied, ' There were thirteen people drowned yesterday evening out of a four-oared boat.' That proved that the boat I had seen at 12.30 P.M. was a vision foreshadowing the wreck of the boat off Darby's Garden at 5.30 P.M. The position, shape, and size of the boat seen by me were identical with the one that was lost on the evening of May 18, 1902."

The second story relates how a lady witnessed a vision (shall we call it) of a suicide a week before the terrible deed was committed. This incident surely makes it clear that such cannot be looked upon as special interventions of Providence, for if the lady had recognised the man, she might have prevented his rash act. Mrs. MacAlpine says: " In June 1889, I drove to Castleblaney, in Co. Monaghan, to meet my sister: I expected her at three o'clock, but as she did not come by that train, I put up the horse and went for a walk in the demesne. At length becoming tired, I sat down on a rock by the edge of a lake. My attention was quite taken up with the beauty of the scene before me, as it was a glorious summer's day. Presently I felt a cold chill creep through me, and a curious stiffness came over my limbs, as if I could not move, though wishing to do so. I felt frightened, yet chained to the spot, and as if impelled to stare at the water straight before me. Gradually a black cloud seemed to rise, and in the midst of it I saw a tall man, in a tweed suit, jump into the water and sink. In a moment the darkness was gone, and I again became sensible of the heat and sunshine, but I was awed and felt eerie. This happened about June 25, and on July 3 a Mr. ——, a bank clerk, committed suicide by drowning himself in the lake." [1]

The following incident occurred in the United States, but, as it is closely connected with this country, it will not seem out of place to insert it here. It is sent by Mr. Richard Hogan, as the personal experience of his sister, Mrs. Mary Murnane, and is given in her own words.

" On the 4th of August 1886, at 10.30 o'clock in the morning, I left my own house, 21 Montrose Street, Philadelphia, to do some shopping. I had not proceeded more than fifty yards when on turning the corner of the street I observed my aunt approaching me within five or six yards. I was greatly astonished, for the last letter I had from home (Limerick) stated that she was dying of consumption, but the thought occurred to me that she might have recovered somewhat and come out to Philadelphia. This opinion was quickly changed as we approached each other, for our eyes met, and she had the colour of one who had risen from the grave. I seemed to feel my hair stand on end, for just as we were about to

[1] *Proceedings S.P.R. x.* 332.

pass each other she turned her face towards me, and I gasped, ' My God, she is dead, and is going to speak to me! ' but no word was spoken, and she passed on. After proceeding a short distance I looked back, and she continued on to Washington Avenue, where she disappeared from me. There was no other person near at the time, and being so close, I was well able to note what she wore. She held a sunshade over her head, and the clothes, hat, etc., were those I knew so well before I left Ireland. I wrote home telling what I had seen, and asking if she was dead. I received a reply saying she was not dead at the date I saw her, but had been asking if a letter had come from me for some days before her death. It was just two days before she actually died that I had seen her."

A gentleman sends the following account of an experience, a premonition of death, which was shared by his friend, and which can hardly be attributed to natural causes.

" The incident I am about to relate occurred in the year 1918 about twenty to one in the morning. It was soft and fine, and not very dark, in fact it was just such a night as one would expect at the period, which was mid-September.

" My occupation at this time was that of engine-cleaner, at which I worked with two comrades in an engine-shed about a quarter of a mile from the local railway station. Our hours of duty were from 7 P.M. to 7 A.M., and at the time the incident which I am about to relate occurred I had done three years of this continuous night-work. I mention this fact, as it will set aside any suspicion that I might have been in any way 'nervy' of the darkness or anything else; as it happens, the dark night was our actual day! It was my usual custom to go every night for a can of clean water from a pump on the town side of the station. On the left one would pass a public-house, while on the right was a graveyard.

" On this particular night I went for the water as usual, and was accompanied on this errand by a friend, another cleaner. It was, as I have said, about twenty to one. The night was unusually still and quiet, a fact which we remarked to each other in the course of conversation. We went along, and just as we were passing the cemetery a heavy gust of wind, with a mournful wailing sound, suddenly sprang up and seemed to catch us in the back. We stopped dead just opposite the graveyard gate, and looked about us. How long we remained there I cannot say, but the wind ceased just as suddenly as it had commenced. I glanced at my friend, and saw that he was as white as a sheet, and he afterwards told me that I myself looked exactly the same.

" On we went without a word. Ten yards more brought us opposite the public-house, which was then owned by a Mrs. B., whose husband had died six months previously after a short illness, and was buried in the graveyard on our right.

APPARITIONS BEFORE DEATH

This house had two doors, one opening on the street through which we were passing, while the other was in a side street which led off this one. We were going by the house when suddenly we heard a terribly heavy knocking at the side door. I stopped immediately, and looked up that street, but nothing could be seen. We were just moving on again when from the side street there came terrible crying, as if a dog were in awful agony or were being severely punished. We went on and filled our can at the pump, and then returned to the engine-shed without any further incident.

"When I came off duty I returned home and went to bed. About mid-day I was awakened by some of the family who told me that Mrs. B. (the owner of the public-house) had had a stroke early that morning, and had died a couple of hours later."

www.ingramcontent.com/pod-product-compliance
Lightning Source LLC
Chambersburg PA
CBHW030543180626
46810CB00005B/1989